Izaak Walton

Waltoniana

Inedited remains in verse and prose of Izaak Walton

Izaak Walton

Waltoniana
Inedited remains in verse and prose of Izaak Walton

ISBN/EAN: 9783337369002

Printed in Europe, USA, Canada, Australia, Japan

Cover: Foto ©Andreas Hilbeck / pixelio.de

More available books at **www.hansebooks.com**

𝔚altoniana

INEDITED REMAINS IN VERSE AND

PROSE OF IZAAK WALTON

AUTHOR OF THE COMPLETE ANGLER

WITH NOTES AND PREFACE

BY

RICHARD HERNE SHEPHERD

LONDON
PICKERING AND CO.
196 PICCADILLY
1878

CONTENTS.

CONTENTS.

PREFACE.

FEW men who have written books have been able to win fo large a fhare of the perfonal affection of their readers as honeft Izaak Walton has done, and few books are laid down with fo genuine a feeling of regret as the "Complete Angler" certainly is, that they are no longer. "One of the gentleft and tendereft fpirits of the feventeenth century," we all know his dear old face, with its cheerful, happy, ferene look, and we fhould all have liked to accompany him on one of thofe angling excurfions from Tottenham High Crofs, and to have liftened to the quaint, garrulous, fportive talk, the outcome of a religion which was like his homely garb, not too good for every-day wear. We fee him, now diligent in his bufinefs, now commemorating the virtues of that clufter of fcholars and

b   churchmen

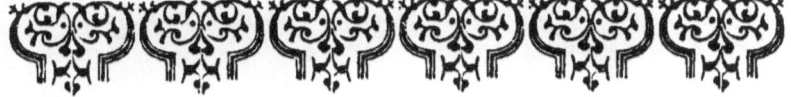

PREFACE.

churchmen with whofe friendfhip he was favoured in youth, and teaching his young brother-in-law, Thomas Ken, to walk in their faintly footfteps, —now bufy with his rod and line, or walking and talking with a friend, ftaying now and then to quaff an honeft glafs at a wayfide ale-houfe— leading a fimple, cheerful, blamelefs life

> " 'Thro' near a century of pleafant years." *

* " Happy old man, whofe worth all mankind knows
   Except himfelf, who charitably fhows
   The ready road to Virtue, and to Praife,
   The road to many long, and happy days ;
   The noble arts of generous piety,
   And how to compafs true felicity.
   —— he knows no anxious cares,
   Thro' near a Century of pleafant years ;
   Eafy he lives and cheerful fhall he die,
   Well fpoken of by late pofterity."
June 5, 1683.
(*Flatman's Commendatory Verfes prefixed to " Thealma and Clearchus ;" Poems and Songs by Thomas Flatman, Third Edition.*)

We

PREFACE.

We have faid that the reader regrets that Walton fhould have left fo little behind him : his "Angler" and his Lives are all that is known to moft. But we are now enabled to prefent thofe who love his memory with a collection of fugitive pieces, in verfe and profe, extending in date of compofition over a period of fifty years,—beginning with the Elegy on Donne, in 1633, and terminating only with his death in 1683. All thefe, however unambitious, are more or lefs characteriftic of the man, and impregnated with the fame fpirit of genial piety that diftinguifhes the two well-known books to which they form a fupplement.

Walton's devotion to literature muft have begun at an early age ; for in a little poem, entitled *The Love of Amos and Laura*, publifhed in 1619, when he was only twenty-fix, and attributed varioufly to Samuel Purchas, author of " The Pilgrims," and to Samuel Page, we find the following dedication to him :—

" To

PREFACE.

"To my approved
and much respec-
ted friend, Iz. Wa.

" To thee, thou more then thrice beloved friend,
I too unworthy of so great a blisse :
These harsh-tun'd lines I here to thee commend,
Thou being cause it is now as it is :
　　For hadst thou held thy tongue, by silence might
　　These have beene buried in obliuious night.

" If they were pleasing, I would call them thine,
And disauow my title to the verse :
But being bad, I needes must call them mine.
No ill thing can be cloathed in thy verse.
　　Accept them then, and where I have offended,
　　Rase thou it out, and let it be amended.

　　　　　　　　　　　　　　　　" S. P."*

What poems Walton wrote in his youth, we
have now no means of knowing; it has not been

---

* *The Love of Amos and Laura.   Written by S. P. London
Printed for Richard Hawkins, dwelling in Chancery-Lane, neere
Serieants Inne,* 1619. Printed at the end of a volume entitled,
Alcilia, Philoparthens louing Folly, &c., which, from its being

　　　　　　　　　　　　　　　　discovered

PREFACE.

difcovered that any have been printed, unlefs we adopt the theory advocated by Mr. Singer,* and by a writer in the " Retrofpective Review," † that the poem of *Thealma and Clearchus*, which he publifhed in the laft year of his life, as a pofthumous fragment of his relation John Chalkhill, was really a juvenile work of his own. Some plaufibility is lent to this notion by the faɛt that Walton fpeaks of the author with fo much reticence and referve in his preface to the volume,

figned at the end with the initials " J. C.," has been attributed to Walton's friend, John Chalkhill, whofe pofthumous poem, *Thealma and Clearchus*, he publifhed in the laft year of his life. The lines to Walton do not appear in the earlier quarto edition of the book iffued by the fame publifher in 1613, or in the later quarto of 1628.

* *Thealma and Clearchus: a Paftoral Romance, by John Chalkhill. Firft Publifhed by Ifaac Walton*, 1683. *A New Edition. Revifed and Correɛted (by S. W. Singer). Chifwick:* 1820.

† Vol. iv. (1821), pp. 230-249.

and

PREFACE.

and alſo that in introducing two of Chalkhill's ſongs into the "Complete Angler," he does not beſtow on them the cuſtomary words of commendation. This theory has been rebutted by others, who aſſert that Walton was of too truthful and guileleſs a nature to reſort to ſuch an artifice. We confeſs that we are unable to ſee anything diſhoneſt in the adoption, as a pſeudonym, of the name of a deceaſed friend, or anything more than Walton appears to have done on another occaſion when he publiſhed his two letters on "Love and Truth." It is certain, however, that a family of Chalkhills exiſted, with whom Walton was cloſely connected by his marriage with the ſiſter of Biſhop Ken. But that an "acquaintant and friend of Edmund Spenſer," capable of writing ſuch a poem as *Thealma and Clearchus*, ſhould have kept his talents ſo concealed, that in an age of commendatory verſes no ſlighteſt contemporary record of him exiſts—is, to ſay the leaſt, extraordinary.

PREFACE.

extraordinary. There are cogent arguments then
on both fides of the queſtion, and there is very
little poſitive proof on either: ſo we muſt be
content to leave the matter in ſome doubt and
obſcurity.

The firſt produćtion to which our author
attached the well-known ſignature of " Iz. Wa."
was an. Elegy on the Death of Dr. Donne, the
Dean of St. Paul's, prefixed to a collećtion of
Donne's Poems. Walton was then forty years
of age. From this time forward we find him
more or leſs engaged, at not very long intervals,
on literary labours, till the very year of his
death.

The care which Walton ſpent on his produc-
tions ſeems to have been very great. He wrote
and re-wrote, correćted, amended, refcinded, and
added. This very poem—the Elegy on Donne
—he completely remodelled in his old age, when
he inſerted it in the collećtion of his Lives.
But

PREFACE.

But we have thought it well to give the original verfion here as a literary curiofity, and the firft work of his that has come down to us. The original Lives themfelves — efpecially thofe of Wotton and Donne—were mere sketches of what they are in their prefent enlarged form.

Walton had the good fortune to be thrown very early in life into the fociety and intimacy of men who were his fuperiors in rank and education. But he had enough of culture, joined to his inherent reverence of mind, to appreciate and underftand all that they had and he wanted.

The preface to Sir John Skeffington's *Heroe of Lorenzo* had for two centuries lain forgotten, and efcaped the notice of Walton's biographers, till in 1852 it was difcovered by Dr. Blifs of Oxford, and communicated by him to the late William Pickering.

The original Spanifh work was firft publifhed in 1630. The author's real name was not Lorenzo,

PREFACE.

Lorenzo, but Balthazar Gracian, a Jefuit of Aragon, who flourifhed during the firft half of the feventeenth century, when the cultivated ftyle took poffeffion of Spanifh profe, and rofe to its greateft confideration.* It is a collection of fhort, wife apothegms and maxims for the conduct of life, fometimes illuftrated by ftories of valour, or prowefs, or magnanimity, of the old Caftilian heroes who figure in "Count Lucanor." The book, though now no longer read, muft have been very popular at one time, for there exift two or three later Englifh verfions of it, without, however, the nervous concentration of ftyle and idiomatic diction that characterize the tranflation fent forth to the world under Walton's aufpices.

The two Letters publifhed in 1680 under the

---

* Ticknor's *Hiftory of Spanifh Literature* (Lond. 1849), vol. iii. p. 177.

title

PREFACE.

title of Love and Truth,* were written refpec-
tively in the years 1668 and 1679. The evidence
of their authorfhip is twofold, and we think
quite conclufive. In one of the very few copies
known to exift, and now in the library of Emanuel
College, Cambridge, its original poffeffor, Arch-
bifhop Sancroft, has written :—" Is. Walton's 2
letters conc. yᵉ Diftempˢ. of yᵉ Times, 1680,"
and Dr. Zouch appended to his reprint of the

---

* *Love and Truth :* | *in* | *Two modeft and peaceable* | *Letters* |
concerning | *The diftempers of the prefent Times.* | *Written* |
From a quiet and Conformable Citizen of | London, *to two*
bufie and Factious | *Shop-keepers in Coventry.* |

1 Pet. 4. 15.
But let none of you fuffer as a bufiebody in other mens/
matters./

London,/ Printed by *M. C.* for *Henry Brome* at the Gun/
in St. *Pauls* Church-yard. 1680.

Collation : 4to. pp. iv. (with Title) 40 (Sig. A 1 and 2 ;
B to E 4).

tract

PREFACE.

tract * a number of parallel paſſages from other acknowledged writings of Walton, of themſelves almoſt ſufficient to fix the queſtion on internal evidence alone.

In the Britiſh Muſeum copy of this tract is the following note on one of the fly-leaves in the autograph of the late William Pickering :—

"The preſent is the only copy I have met with after twenty years' ſearch, excepting the one in Emanuel College, Cambridge. W. Pickering."

The copy deſcribed above [*i.e.*, the Emanuel College copy] appears to be the ſame edition as the preſent [that now in the Britiſh Muſeum], but has the following variation. After the title-page is printed

The Author to the Stationer

"Mr. Brome," &c., and the Epiſtle ends with

* York, 1795, pp. x. 70.

"Your

PREFACE.

"Your friend," without the N. N. which is found in this copy. But what is more remarkable, the printed word Author is run through, and corrected with a pen, and over it written *Publisher*, which is evidently in the handwriting of Walton. So Mr. Pickering further certifies.

The following allusion towards the bottom of p. 37 confirms the idea of Walton's authorship. Speaking of Hugh Peters and John Lilbourn, the writer says :—" Their turbulent lives and uncomfortable deaths are not I hope yet worn out of the memory of many. He that compares them with the holy life and happy death of Mr. George Herbert, as it is plainly and *I hope truly* writ by Mr. Isaac Walton, may in it find a perfect pattern for an humble and devout Christian to imitate," &c.

The following are the chief parallel passages in this pamphlet and in Walton's other writings, as indicated by Zouch :—

Second

PREFACE.

Second Letter, p. 19.

I wiſh as heartily as you do that all ſuch Clergy-mens Wives as have ſilk Cloaths be-daubed with Lace, and their heads hanged about with painted Ribands, were enjoyned Penance for their pride: And their Huſbands puniſht for being ſo tame, or ſo lovingly-ſimple, as to ſuffer them; for, by ſuch Cloaths, they proclaim their own Ambition, and their Huſbands folly.

And I ſay the like, concerning their *ſtriving for Precedency.*

P. 20.

And, I confeſs alſo, what you ſay of a Clergy-mans bidding *to faſt* on the Eves of Holy-days, in Lent, and the *Ember Weeks:* And I wiſh thoſe biddings were forborn, or better practiſed by themſelves.

Life of George Herbert.

Mr. George Herbert having changed his ſword and ſilk clothes into a canonical coat, thus warned Mⁿ. Herbert againſt this egregious folly of *ſtriving for precedency:*——"You are now a miniſter's wife, and muſt now ſo far forget your father's houſe, as not to claim a precedence of any of your pariſhioners," &c.

Life of George Herbert.

One cure for the wickedneſs of the times would be, for the clergy themſelves to keep the Ember-weeks ſtrictly, &c.

P. 20.

PREFACE.

P. 20.

And, I wish as heartily as you can, that they would not only read, but pray, the Common Prayer; and not huddle it up so fast (as too many do) by getting into a middle of a second Collect, before a devout Hearer can say Amen to the first.

Life of George Herbert.

Those ministers that huddled up the church prayers without a visible reverence and affection: namely, such as seemed to say the Lord's Prayer or a collect in a breath.

P. 20.

And now, having unbowelled my very soul thus freely to you, &c.

Preface to Sanderson's XXI Sermons, 1655.

But since I had thus adventured to unbowel myself, and to lay open the very inmost thoughts of my heart.

P. 21.

A Corrosive, or (as *Solomon* says of ill-gotten riches) *like gravel in his teeth.*

Life of Sanderson.

Riches so gotten, and added to his great estate, would prove *like gravel in his teeth.*

P. 21.

Those *Bishops* and *Martyrs*

Life of Sir H. Wotton.

It was the advice of Sir that

PREFACE.

that assisted in this Reformation, did not (as Sir *Henry Wotton* said wisely) think *the farther* they went from the Church of Rome, the nearer they got to heaven.

Henry Wotton, "Take heed of thinking the farther you go from the Church of Rome, the nearer you are to God."

P. 23.

To make the Women, the Shop-keepers, and the middle-witted People . . . less busie, and more humble and lowly in their own eyes, and to think that they are neither called, nor are fit to meddle with, and judge of the most hidden and mysterious points in *Divinity*, and Government of the *Church* and *State*.

Life of Richard Hooker.

Here the very women and shopkeepers were able to judge of predestination, and determine what laws were fit to be obeyed or abolished.

P. 36.

I desire you to look back with me to the beginning of the late Long Parliament 1640, at which time we were the quietest and happiest people in the Christian World.

Life of Sanderson.

Some years before the unhappy Long Parliament, this nation being then happy and in peace.

To

PREFACE.

To the prefent Editor the collection and annotation of thefe Remains has been a moft welcome labour of love. Some of his oldeft and moft cherifhed memories connect themfelves with the author of the "Complete Angler." That book was one of the firft that he ever read with real and genuine delight; and even before reading days commenced, in the earlieft dawn of memory, the place where Walton had cut his familiar fignature of " Iz. Wa." on Chaucer's tomb in Weftminfter Abbey, was pointed out to him often by a kindred fpirit now here no more. The name of Walton will alfo be found enfhrined in the earlieft profe production * to which the Editor prefixed his own name.

R. H. S.

* *The School of Pantagruel*, Sunbury, 1862, p. 9.

AN ELEGIE UPON D^R. DONNE.

1633.

B *[Juvenilia:*

[*Juvenilia: or Certaine Paradoxes and Problemes, written
by I. Donne. London, Printed by E. P. for Henry Seyle, and
are to be fold at the figne of the Tygers head, in Saint Pauls
Church-yard, Anno Dom.* 1633 (pp. 382-384).

*Poems, by J. D. with Elegies on the Author's Death.
London Printed by M. F. for* JOHN MARRIOT, *and are to be
fold at his Shop in S*. *Dunftans Church-yard in Fleet-ftreet,*
1635.

The text is printed from the revifed verfion of 1635, and
the original readings of 1633 are given at the foot of the
page.]

An

An Elegie upon D^R. Donne.

UR *Donne* is dead ; England fhould
mourne, may fay
We had a man where language chofe
to ftay
And fhew her gracefull power.[1] I would not praife
That and his vaſt wit (which in thefe vaine dayes
Make many proud) but, as they ferv'd to unlock
That Cabinet, his minde : where fuch a ftock
Of knowledge was repof'd, as all lament
(Or fhould) this generall caufe of difcontent.
 And I rejoyce I am not fo fevere,
But (as I write a line) to weepe a teare

[1] In the edition of 1633, the poem opens thus :—
 Is *Donne*, great *Donne* deceaſ'd ? then England fay
 Thou'haſt loſt a man where language chofe to ftay
 And fhew it's gracefull power, &c.

For

For his deceafe; Such fad extremities
May make fuch men as I write Elegies.
   And wonder not; for, when a generall loffe
Falls on a nation, and they flight the croffe,
God hath raif'd Prophets to awaken them
From ftupifaction; witneffe my milde pen,
Not uf'd to upbraid the world, though now it muft
Freely and boldly, for, the caufe is juft.
   Dull age, Oh I would fpare thee, but th'art worfe,
Thou art not onely dull, but haft a curfe
Of black ingratitude; if not, couldft thou
Part with *miraculous Donne*, and make no vow
For thee, and thine, fucceffively to pay
A fad remembrance to his dying day?
   Did his youth fcatter *Poetry*, wherein
Was all Philofophy? was every finne,
Character'd in his *Satyrs?* Made fo foule
That fome have fear'd their fhapes, and kept their
    foule
Safer by reading verfe? Did he give *dayes*

                              Paft

WALTONIANA.

Paſt marble monuments, to thoſe, whoſe praiſe
He would perpetuate? Did he (I feare
The dull will doubt:) theſe at his twentieth year?
  But, more matur'd; Did his full ſoule conceive,
And in harmonious-holy-numbers weave
A **Crown of ſacred ſonnets*, fit to adorne **La Corona.*
A dying Martyrs brow: or, to be worne
On that bleſt head of *Mary Magdalen,*
After ſhe wip'd Chriſts feet, but not till then?
Did hee (fit for ſuch penitents as ſhee
And he to uſe) leave us a *Litany,*
Which all devout men love, and ſure, it ſhall,
As times grow better, grow more claſſicall?
Did he write *Hymnes*, for piety, for wit,[1]
Equall to thoſe, great grave *Prudentius* writ?
Spake he all *Languages?* knew he all Lawes?
The grounds and uſe of *Phyſick;* but becauſe
'Twas mercenary, wav'd it? Went to ſee

---

[1] for piety and wit,—1633.

That

That bleſſed place of *Chriſts nativity?*
Did he returne and preach him? preach him ſo
As ſince S. *Paul* none did, none could? Thoſe know,
(Such as were bleſt to heare him) this is truth.[1]
Did he confirm thy aged?[2] convert thy youth?
Did he theſe wonders? And is this deare loſſe
Mourn'd by ſo few? (few for ſo great a croſſe.)
    But ſure the ſilent are ambitious all
To be Cloſe Mourners at his Funerall;
If not; In common pitty they forbare
By repetitions to renew our care;
Or, knowing, griefe conceiv'd, conceal'd, conſumes
Man irreparably, (as poyſon'd fumes
Doe waſte the braine) make ſilence a ſafe way,
To' inlarge the Soule from theſe walls, mud and clay,
(Materials of this body) to remaine
With *Donne* in heaven, where no promiſcuous pain

[1] As none but hee did, or could do? They know
    (Such as were bleſt to heare him know) 'tis truth.—1633.
[2] *age* in the edition of 1633.

Leſſens

Leffens the joy we have, for, with *him*, all
Are fatisfy'd with *joyes effentiall.*
    Dwell on this joy my thoughts; oh, doe not call[1]
Griefe back, by thinking of his Funerall;
Forget hee lov'd mee; Wafte not my fad yeares;
(Which haft to *Davids* feventy,) fill'd with feares
And forrow for his death; Forget his parts,
Which finde a living grave in good mens hearts;
And, (for, my firft is dayly payd for finne)
Forget to pay my fecond figh for him:
Forget his powerfull preaching; and forget
I am his *Convert.* Oh my frailty! let
My flefh be no more heard, it will obtrude
This lethargy: fo fhould my gratitude,
My flowes[2] of gratitude fhould fo be broke;
Which can no more be, than *Donnes* vertues fpoke
By any but himfelfe; for which caufe, I

---

[1] My thoughts, Dwell on this *Joy*, and do not call—1633.
[2] *vowes* in the edition of 1633.

Write

WALTONIANA.

Write no *Encomium*, but this *Elegie*,[1]
Which, as a free-will-offring, I here give
Fame, and the world, and parting with it grieve
I want abilities, fit to fet forth
A monument, great, as Donnes matchleffe worth.

Iz. W<small>A</small>.

[1] Write no *Encomium*, but an *Elegie*.
Here the poem clofed in the edition of 1633.

LINES

LINES ON A PORTRAIT OF DONNE IN HIS EIGHTEENTH YEAR.

1635.

[Engraved

[Engraved under William Marſhall's Portrait of Donne,
" Anno Dñi. 1591.   Ætatis ſuæ 18," prefixed to the ſecond
edition of Donne's Poems, 1635.]

On a Portrait of DONNE *taken in his eighteenth year.*

THIS was for youth, Strength, Mirth, and
wit that Time
Moſt count their golden Age; but
t'was not thine.
Thine was thy later yeares, ſo much refind
From youths Droſſe, Mirth & wit; as thy pure
mind
Thought (like the Angels) nothing but the Praiſe
Of thy Creator, in thoſe laſt, beſt Dayes.
Witnes this Booke, (thy Embleme) which begins
With Love; but endes, with Sighes, & Teares
for ſiñs.

Iz: Wa:

COMMENDATORY VERSES PREFIXED TO THE MERCHANTS MAPPE OF COMMERCE.

1638.

[The

[The Merchants Mappe of Commerce : wherein the Universall Manner and Matter of Trade, is compendiously handled. By Lewes Roberts, Merchant. At London, Printed by R. O. for Ralph Mabb MDCXXXVIII. *fol.*

——— The Second Edition, Corrected and much Enlarged. London, MDCLXXI. *fol.*]

In

*In praiſe of my friend the Author,
and his Booke.*

To the Reader.

If thou would'ſt be a *States-man*, and
  ſurvay
  Kingdomes for information; heres a
  way
Made plaine, and eaſie: fitter far for thee
Then great *Ortelius* his *Geographie.*

If thou would'ſt be a *Gentleman*, in more
Then title onely; this Map yeelds thee ſtore
Of Obſervations, fit for Ornament,
Or uſe, or to give curious eares content.

         If

WALTONIANA.

If thou would'ſt be a *Merchant*, buy this Booke :
For 'tis a prize worth gold ; and doe not looke
Daily for ſuch disburſements ; no, 'tis rare,
And ſhould be caſt up with thy richeſt ware.

READER, if thou be any, or all three ;
(For theſe may meet and make a harmonie)
Then prayſe this Author for his uſefull paines,
Whoſe aime is publike good, not private gaines.

Iz. WA.

PREFACE

PREFACE TO QUARLES'S SHEPHERDS

ORACLES.

1645.

[The Shepheards Oracles : Delivered in Certain Eglogues. By Fra : Quarles. London, Printed by M. F. for
John Marriot and Richard Marriot, and are to be fold at
their fhop in S. Dunftans Church-yard Fleetftreet, under the
Dyall. 1646.]

To

WALTONIANA.

To the Reader.

READER,

THOUGH the Authour had some years before his lamented death, compos'd, review'd, and corrected these Eglogues; yet, he left no Epistle to the Reader, but onely a Title, and a blanke leafe for that purpose.

Whether he meant some Allegoricall exposition of the Shepheards names, or their Eglogues, is doubtfull : but 'tis certain, that as they are, they appear a perfect pattern of the Authour; whose person, and minde, were both lovely, and his conversation such as distill'd pleasure, knowledge, and vertue, into his friends and acquaintance.

'Tis confest, these Eglogues are not so wholly divine as many of his publisht Meditations, which
speak

ſpeak *his affeĉtions to be ſet upon things that are above*, and yet even ſuch men have their intermitted howres, and (as their company gives occaſion) com-mixtures of heavenly and earthly thoughts.

You are therefore requeſted to fancy him caſt by fortune into the company of ſome yet unknown Shepheards : and you have a liberty to beleeve 'twas by this following accident.

" He in a Sommers morning (about that howre
" when the great eye of Heaven first opens it ſelfe
" to give light to us mortals) walking a gentle pace
" towards a Brook (whoſe Spring-head was not far
" diſtant from his peacefull habitation) fitted with
" Angle, Lines, and Flyes : Flyes proper for that
" ſeaſon (being the fruitfull Month of *May;*) in-
" tending all diligence to beguile the timorous
" Trout, (with which that watry element
" abounded) obſerv'd a more then common con-
" courſe of Shepheards, all bending their unwearied
" ſteps towards a pleaſant Meadow within his preſent

" fent profpect, and had his eyes made more happy
" to behold the two fair Shepheardeffes *Amaryllis*
" and *Aminta* ftrewing the foot-paths with Lillies,
" and Ladyfmocks, fo newly gathered by their
" fair hands, that they yet fmelt more fweet then
" the morning, and immediately met (attended
" with *Clora Clorinda*, and many other Wood-
" nymphs) the fair and yertuous *Parthenia :* who
" after a courteous falutation and inquiry of his
" intended Journey, told him the neighbour-Shep-
" heards of that part of Arcadia had dedicated that
" day to be kept holy to the honour of their great
" God *Pan ;* and, that they had defigned her Mis-
" treffe of a Love-feaft, which was to be kept that
" prefent day, in an Arbour built that morning, for
" that purpofe ; fhe told him alfo, that *Orpheus*
" would bee there, and bring his Harp, *Pan* his
" Pipe, and *Titerus* his Oaten-reed, to make mufick
" at this feaft ; fhee therefore perfwaded him, not to
" lofe, but change that dayes pleafure ; before he
could

" could return an anfwer they were unawares en-
" tred into a living moving Lane, made of Shep-
" heards and Pilgrimes; who had that morning
" meafured many miles to be eye-witneffes of that
" days pleafure; this Lane led them into a large
" Arbour, whofe wals were made of the yeelding
" Willow, and fmooth Beech boughs : and covered
" over with Sycamore leaves, and Honyfuccles."

I might now tell in what manner (after her firſt
entrance into this Arbour) *Philoclea* (*Philoclea* the
fair *Arcadian* Shepheardeffe) crown'd her Temples
with a Garland, with what flowers, and by whom
'twas made; I might tell what guefts (befides
Aftrea and *Adonis*) were at this feaſt; and who
(befide *Mercury*) waited at the Table, this I might
tell : but may not, cannot expreffe what muſick
the Gods and Wood-nymphs made within; and
the Linits, Larks, and Nightingales about this
Arbour, during this holy day : which began in
harmleffe mirth, and (for *Bacchus* and his gang
were

were abſent) ended in love and peace, which *Pan* (for he onely can doe it) continue in *Arcadia, and reſtore to the diſturbed Iſland of* Britannia, *and grant that each honeſt Shepheard may again ſit under his own Vine and Fig-tree, and feed his own flock, and with love enjoy the fruits of peace, and be more thankfull.*

Reader, at this time and place, the Authour contracted a friendſhip with certain ſingle-hearted Shepheards : with whom (as he return'd from his River-recreations) he often reſted himſelfe, and whileſt in the calm evening their flocks fed about them, heard that diſcourſe, which (with the Shepheards names) is preſented in theſe Eglogues.

23 Novem. 1645.

COUPLET ON DR. RICHARD SIBBES.

1650.

[Written

[Written by Izaak Walton in his copy of D^r. Richard Sibbes's work, *The Returning Backflider*, 4to., 1650, preferved in the Cathedral Library, Salifbury. See Sir Harris Nicolas' Memoir of Walton, clv.]

Of

WALTONIANA.

O F this bleſt man let this juſt praiſe be
given,
Heaven was in him, before he was in
heaven.

IZAAK WALTON.

DEDICATION OF RELIQUIÆ
WOTTONIANÆ.

1651.

[Reliquiæ

[Reliquiæ Wottonianæ, or, a Collection of Lives, Letters, Poems ; with Characters of Sundry Personages : and other Incomparable Pieces of Language and Art.   By The curious Penfil of the Ever Memorable Sr. Henry Wotton, Kt., Late, Provoft of Eton Colledg.   London, Printed by Thomas Maxey, for R. Marriot, G. Bedel, and T. Garthwait. 1651.]

To

WALTONIANA.

To the Right Honourable The Lady Mary Wotton Baronnefs, and to her Three Noble Daughters.

THE LADY $\left\{\begin{array}{l}\text{KATHERIN STANHOP.} \\ \text{MARGARET TUFTON.} \\ \text{ANN HALES.}\end{array}\right.$

SINCE Bookes feeme by cuftome to Challenge a dedicatiõ, Juftice would not allow, that what either was, or con-cern'd Sir Henry Wotton, fhould be appropriated to any other Perfons; Not only for that nearneffe of Aliance and Blood (by which you may chalenge a civil right to what was his;) but, by

by a title of that intireneſſe of Affection, which was in you to each other, when Sir Henry Wotton had a being upon Earth.

And ſince yours was a Friendſhip made up of generous Principles, as I cannot doubt but theſe indeavours to preſerve his Memory wil be acceptable to all that lov'd him; ſo eſpecially to you : from whom I have had ſuch incouragements as hath imboldned me to this Dedication. Which you are moſt humbly intreated may be accepted from

Your very reall ſervant,

I. W.

On

ON THE DEATH OF WILLIAM CARTWRIGHT.

1651.

[Comedies, Tragi-Comedies, with other Poems, by Mr.
William Cartwright, late Student of Chrift-Church in Oxford, and Proctor of the Univerfity. London, Printed for
Humphrey Mofeley, and are to be fold at his Shop, at the
fign of the Prince's Arms in St. Pauls Church-yard, 1651.]

 On

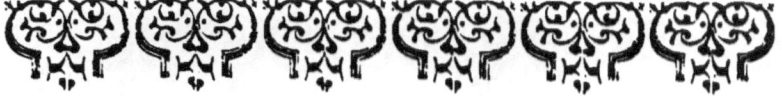

WALTONIANA.

On the Death of my dear Friend Mr. William Cartwright, relating to the foregoing Elegies.

I CANNOT keep my purpose, but muſt give
  Sorrow and Verſe their way ; nor will I grieve
Longer in ſilence ; no, that poor, poor part
Of natures legacy, Verſe void of Art,
And undiſſembled teares, CARTWRIGHT ſhall have
Fixt on his Hearſe ; and wept into his grave.
 Muſes I need you not ; for, Grief and I
Can in your abſence weave an Elegy :
Which we will do ; and often inter-weave
Sad Looks, and Sighs ; the ground-work muſt receive
Such Characters, or be adjudg'd unfit
For my Friends ſhroud ; others have ſhew'd their
  Wit,   Learning,

WALTONIANA.

Learning, and Language fitly; for thefe be
Debts due to his great Merits : but for me,
My aymes are like my felf, humble and low,
Too mean to fpeak his praife, too mean to fhow
The World what it hath loft in lofing thee,
Whofe Words and Deeds were perfect Harmony.
    But now 'tis loft; loft in the filent Grave,
Loft to us Mortals, loft, 'till we fhall have
Admiffion to that Kingdom, where He fings
Harmonious Anthems to the King of Kings.
    Sing on bleft Soul! be as thou wast below,
A more than common inftrument to fhow
Thy Makers praife; fing on, whilft I lament
Thy lofs, and court a holy difcontent,
With fuch pure thoughts as thine, to dwell with me,
Then I may hope to live, and dye like thee,
To live belov'd, dye mourn'd, thus in my grave;
Bleffings that Kings have wifh'd, but cannot have.

Iz. WA.

PREFACE

PREFACE TO SIR JOHN SKEFFINGTON'S

HEROE OF LORENZO.

1652.

The

[The Heroe, of Lorenzo, or, The way to Eminencie and
Perfeƈtion. A piece of ferious Spanifh wit Originally in
that language written, and in Englifh. By Sir John Skeffington, Kt. and Barronet. London, printed for John Martin
and James Alleftrye at the Bell in St Pauls Church-yard.
1652.]

Let

WALTONIANA.

Let this be told the Reader,

THAT Sir *John Skeffington* (one of his late Majefties fervants, and a ftranger to no language of *Chriftendom*) did about 40 years now paft, bring this *Hero* out of *Spain* into *England*.

There they two kept company together 'till about 12 months now paft : and then, in a retyrement of that learned knights (by reafon of a fequeftration for his mafters caufe) a friend coming to vifit him, they fell accidentally into a difcourfe of the *wit* and *galantry* of the *Spanifh Nation*.

That difcourfe occafioned an example or two, to be brought out of this *Hero* : and, thofe examples (with Sir *John's* choice language and illuftration)

tration) were fo relifht by his friend (a ftranger to the *Spanifh tongue*) that he became reftles 'till he got a promife from Sir *John* to tranflate the whole, which he did in a few weeks; and fo long as that imployment lafted it proved an excellent diverfion from his many fad thoughts; But he hath now chang'd that Condition, to be poffeft of that place into which fadneffe is not capable of entrance.

And his abfence from this world hath occafion'd mee (who was one of thofe few that he gave leave to know him, for he was a retyr'd man) to tell the Reader that I heard him fay, he had not made the *Englifh* fo fhort, or few words, as the originall; becaufe in that, the Author had expreft himfelf fo enigmatically, that though he indevour'd to tranflate it plainly; yet, he thought it was not made comprehenfible enough for common Readers, therefore he declar'd to me, that he intended to make it fo by a coment on the margent; which he had begun, but (be it fpoke with forrow) he and
thofe

WALTONIANA.

thofe thoughts are now buried in the filent Grave,[1]
and my felf, with thofe very many that lov'd him,
left to lament that loffe.

I. W.

---

[1] Compare the poem on the death of Cartwright, *fupra :*—
" But now 'tis loft ; loft in the filent grave," &c.

COMMENDATORY VERSES TO THE

AUTHOR OF SCINTILLULA

ALTARIS.

1652.

[Scintillula Altaris or, a Pious Reflection on Primitive Devotion: as to the Feafts and Fafts of the Chriftian Church, Orthodoxally Revived. By Edward Sparke, B.D. London; Printed by T. Maxey for Richard Marriot, and are to be fold at his Shop in S^t. Dunftan's Church-yard in Fleetftreet, 1652.

This book reached a Seventh Edition during Walton's lifetime; but his Commendatory Verfes are only to be found in the firft.]

To

To the Author upon the sight of the first sheet of his Book.

Y worthy friend, I am much pleaſ'd to know,
You have begun to pay the debt you owe

By promiſe, to ſo many pious friends,
In printing your choice Poems; it commends
Both them, and you, that they have been deſir'd
By perſons of ſuch Judgment; and admir'd
They muſt be moſt, by thoſe that beſt ſhal know
What praiſe to holy Poetry we owe.
So ſhall your Diſquiſitions too ; for, there
Choice learning, and bleſt piety, appear.

All　.

WALTONIANA.

All ufefull to poor Chriftians : where they may
Learne Primitive Devotion.   Each Saints day
Stands as a Land-mark in an erring age
to guide fraile mortals in their pilgrimage
To the Cœleftiall *Can'an ;* and each Faft,
Is both the fouls direction, and repaft :
   All fo expreft, that I am glad to know
   You have begun to pay the debt you owe.
Iz. WA.

DEDICATION

DEDICATION OF THE LIFE OF DONNE
AND ADVERTISEMENT TO
THE READER.

1658.

[The

[The Life of John Donne, Dr. in Divinity, and Late Dean of Saint Pauls Church London. The fecond impreffion corrected and enlarged. Ecclus. 48. 14. *He did wonders in his life, and at his death his works were marvelous.* London, Printed by J. G. for R. Marriot, and are to be fold at his fhop under S. Dunftans Church in Fleet-ftreet. 1658.]

To

WALTONIANA.

*To My Noble & honoured Friend Sir Robert
Holt of Aſton, in the County of
Warwick, Baronet.*

Sir,

WHEN this relation of the life of Doctor Donne was firſt made publick, it had beſides the approbation of our late learned & eloquent King, a conjunction with the Authors moſt excellent Sermons to ſupport it; and thus it lay ſome time fortified againſt prejudice; and thoſe paſſions that are by buſie and malicious men too freely vented againſt the dead.

E   And

WALTONIANA.

And yet, now, after almoſt twenty yeares, when though the memory of Dʳ. Donne himſelf, muſt not, cannot die, ſo long as men ſpeak Engliſh; yet when I thought Time had made this relation of him ſo like my ſelf, as to become uſeleſs to the world, and content to be forgotten; I find that a retreat into a deſired privacy, will not be afforded; for the Printers will again expoſe it and me to publick exceptions; and without thoſe ſupports, which we firſt had and needed, and in an Age too, in which Truth & Innocence have not beene able to defend themſelves from worſe then ſevere cenſures.

This I foreſaw, and Nature teaching me ſelfe-preſervation, and my long experience of your abilities aſſuring me that in you it may in found :* to you, Sir, do I make mine addreſſes for an umbrage and protection: and I make it with ſo much humble boldneſſe, as to ſay 'twere degenerous in you not to afford it.

* *Sic:* probably a miſprint for "*be* found ?"—Eᴅ.

For,

WALTONIANA.

For, Sir,

Dʳ. Donne was ſo much a part of yourſelf, as to be incorporated into your Family, by ſo noble a friendſhip, that I may ſay there was a marriage of ſouls betwixt him and your* reverend Grandfather, who in his life was an Angel of our once glorious Church, and now no common Star in heaven.

* *John King,* B. of Lond.

And Dʳ. Donne's love died not with him, but was doubled upon his Heire, your beloved Uncle the Bishop of †Chicheſter, that lives in this froward generation, to be an ornament to his Calling. And this affection to him was by Dʳ. D. ſo teſtified in his life, that he then truſted him with the very ſecrets of his ſoul; & at his death, with what was deareſt to him, even his fame, eſtate, & children.

† *Hen: King,* now B.C.

And you have yet a further title to what was Dʳ. Donne's, by that dear affection & friendſhip
that

that was betwixt him and your parents, by which he entailed a love upon yourſelf, even in your infancy, which was encreaſed by the early teſtimonies of your growing merits, and by them continued, till D. *Donne* put on immortality; and ſo this mortall was turned into a love that cannot die.

And Sir, 'twas pity he was loſt to you in your minority, before you had attained a judgement to put a true value upon the living beauties and elegancies of his converſation; and pitty too, that ſo much of them as were capable of ſuch an expreſſion, were not drawn by the penſil of a *Tytian* or a *Tentoret*, by a pen equall and more laſting then their art; for his life ought to be the example of more then that age in which he died. And yet this copy, though very much, indeed too much ſhort of the Originall, will preſent you with ſome features not unlike your dead friend, and with fewer blemiſhes and more ornaments than when 'twas firſt made publique : which creates a contentment

tentment to my felfe, becaufe it is the more worthy of him, and becaufe I may with more civility intitle you to it.

And in this defigne of doing fo, I have not a thought of what is pretended in moft Dedications, *a Commutation for Courtefies :* no indeed Sir, I put no fuch value upon this trifle; for your owning it will rather increafe my Obligations. But my defire is, that into whofe hands foever this fhall fall, it may to them be a teftimony of my gratitude to your felf and Family, who defcended to fuch a degree of humility as to admit me into their friendfhip in the dayes of my youth; and notwithftanding my many infirmities, have continued me in it till I am become gray-headed; and as Time has added to my yeares, have ftill increafed and multiplied their favours.

This, Sir, is the intent of this Dedication : and having made the declaration of it thus publick, I fhall conclude it with commending them and you to Gods deare love. I

WALTONIANA.

I remain, Sir, what your many merits have made me to be,

   The humbleſt of your Servants,

      ISAAC WALTON.

To

To the Reader.

MY defire is to inform and affure you, that fhall become my Reader, that in that part of this following difcourfe, which is onely narration, I either fpeak my own knowledge, or from the teftimony of fuch as dare do any thing, rather than fpeak an untruth. And for that part of it which is my own obfervation or opinion, if I had a power I would not ufe it to force any mans affent, but leave him a liberty to difbelieve what his own reafon inclines him to.

Next, I am to inform you, that whereas Dᵣ. Donne's life was formerly printed with his Sermons, and then had the fame Preface or Introduction to it; I have not omitted it now, becaufe I have no fuch confidence in what I have done, as to appear without an apology for my undertaking it.

I have faid all when I have wifhed happineffe to my Reader.

I. W.

DAMAN AND DORUS.

An Humble Eglog.

29th may 1660.

[Songs

[Songs and other Poems. By Alex. Brome, Gent. London, Printed for Henry Brome, at the Gun in Ivy-Lane, 1661.
The Second Edition corrected and enlarged, 1664.
The Third Edition enlarged. London, Printed for Henry Brome, at the Star in Little Brittain, 1668.]

To

WALTONIANA.

To my ingenious Friend M^r. Brome, *on his various and excellent Poems: An humble Eglog. Written the 29 of May,* 1660.

Damán *and* Dorus.

DAMAN.

HAIL *happy day! Dorus fit down:
Now let no figh, nor let a frown
Lodge near thy heart, or on thy brow.
The* King! *the* King's *return'd! and now
Let's banifh all fad thoughts and fing*
We have our Laws, and have our King.

Dorus.

WALTONIANA.

DORUS.

'Tis true, and I would sing, but oh !
These wars have sunk my heart so low
'Twill not be rais'd.

DAMAN.

   What not this day ?
Why 'tis the twenty ninth of May :
Let Rebels *spirits sink ; let those*
That like the Goths *and* Vandals *rose*
To ruine families, and bring
Contempt upon our Church, *our* King,
And all that's dear to us, be sad ;
But be not thou, let us be glad.
 And, *Dorus,* to invite thee, look,
Here's a Collection in this Book,
Of all those chearful Songs, that we
Have sung so oft and merilie[1]

[1] Have sung with mirth and merry-gle :—1661.

          As

WALTONIANA.

As we have march'd to fight the caufe
Of *Gods Anointed*, and our *Laws*
Such Songs as make not the leaft ods
Betwixt us *mortals* and the *Gods*:
Such Songs as *Virgins* need not fear
To fing, or a grave *Matron* hear.
Here's *love* dreft *neat*, and *chaft*, and *gay*
As *gardens* in the month of *May*;
Here's harmony, and *Wit*, and *Art*,
To raife thy *thoughts*, and chear thy *heart*.

DORUS.
Written by whom?

DAMAN.
A friend of mine,
And one that's worthy to be thine:
A Civil *fwain*, that knows his times
For bufinefs, and that done makes Rhymes;
But not till then: my Friend's a man
Lov'd by the Mufes; dear to *Pan*:

He

He bleſt him with a chearful heart :
And they with this ſharp wit and Art,
Which he ſo tempers, as no *Swain*,
That's loyal, does or ſhould complain.

Dorus.

I wou'd fain ſee him :

Daman.

    Go with me
Dorus, *to yonder broad* beech-tree,
There we ſhall meet him and Phillis,
Perrigot, *and* Amaryllis,
Tityrus, *and his dear* Clora,
Tom *and* Will, *and their* Paſtora:
There wee'l dance, ſhake hands and ſing,
We have our Laws,
   God bleſs the King.

      Iz. Walton.

       TO

TO MY REVEREND FRIEND THE AUTHOR

OF THE SYNAGOGUE.

1661.

[The

[The Synagogue, or The Shadow of the Temple. Sacred Poems and Private Ejaculations. In imitation of M^r. George Herbert. The fourth Edition corrected and enlarged. London, Printed for Philemon Stephens, at the guilded Lyon in S^t. Pauls Churchyard, 1661. p. 67.]

To

To my Reverend Friend the Author
of the Synagogue.

SIR,

LOV'D you for your Synagogue, before
I knew your perſon ; but now love you
more ;
   Becauſe I find
It is ſo true a picture of your mind :
  Which tunes your ſacred lyre
  To that eternal quire ;
  Where holy *Herbert* ſits
  (O ſhame to prophane wits)
And ſings his and your Anthems, to the praiſe
Of Him that is the firſt and laſt of daies.

Theſe holy Hymns had an Ethereal birth :
For they can raiſe ſad ſouls above the earth

     F   And

WALTONIANA.

And fix them there
Free from the worlds anxieties and fear.
Herbert and you have pow'r
To do this : ev'ry hour
I read you kills a fin,
Or lets a vertue in
To fight againſt it ; and the Holy Ghoſt
Supports my frailties, leſt the day be loſt.

This holy war, taught by your happy pen,
The Prince of Peace approves. When we poor men
Neglect our arms,
W'are circumveſted with a world of harms.
But I will watch, and ward,
And ſtand upon my guard,
And ſtill conſult with you,
And *Herbert*, and renew
My vows, and ſay, Well fare his, and your heart,
The fountains of ſuch ſacred wit and art.

Iz. W<small>A</small>.
EPITAPH

EPITAPH ON HIS SECOND WIFE,

ANNE KEN.

1662.

[In

[In Worcefter Cathedral. The event is thus recorded by Walton in his Family Prayer-Book : " Anne Walton dyed " the 17th of April, about one o'clock in that night, and was " buried in the Virgin Mary's Chapel, in the cathedral in " Worcefter, the 20th day."]

Ex

Ex Terris
M. S.
Here lyeth buried fo much as
could dye of ANNE, the Wife of
Ifaak Walton;
who was
a Woman of Remarkable Prudence,
and of the Primitive Piety; her great
and general knowledge being adorned
with fuch true humility, and bleft
with fo much Chriftian meeknefs, as
made her worthy of a more memorable
Monument.
She dyed! (Alas, that fhe is dead!)
the 17th of April, 1662, aged 52.
Study to be like her.

LETTER TO EDWARD WARD.

1670.

[Preſerved

[Preſerved among the MSS. in the Library of Trinity
College, Dublin.   Firſt printed in "Notes and Queries,"
May 17, 1856.]

ffor

WALTONIANA.

ffor my worthy frend Mᵣ. EDWARD WARD,
  att Rodon Temple, nere vnto Leſter. Att
  Mᵣ. BABINGTONS *att Rodon Temple.*

     Sᵣ.,

I CAME well from Winton to London, about 3 weikes paſt : at that time I left Doᵣ. Hawkins well : and my dafter (after a greate danger of child berth) not very well, but by a late letter from him, I heare they be boeth in good health.

The doctor did tell me a gowne and ſome bookes of yʳˢ were in danger to be loſt, though he had made (at a diſtance) many inquiries after them, and intreated others to doe ſo too, but yet inefectually. He theirfore intreated me to undertake a ſearch : and I have donne it ſo ſuccesfuly that uppon thurſday the 24° inſtant they were d̃d to

that

that letter carryer that Inns at the Rofe in Smith-
feild, and with them the Life of M^r. George Herbert (and 3 others) wrapt up in a paper and
directed to you at Rodon Temple, the booke not
tyed to the bundell, but of it felfe.   The bundell
coft me 3^s. 8^d. carryage to London, and I hope it
will now come fafe to your hands.

What I have to write more is my heartie wifhes
for y^r hapines, for I am

     y^r. affec. frend and feruant,

       Izaak Walton.

Nou^r 26°, 1670.

If you incline to write to me, direct your letter
to be left at Mr Grinfells, a grocer in King ftreite
in Weftminfter.   Much good doe you with the
booke, wch I wifh better.

         DEDICATION

DEDICATION OF THE THIRD EDITION
OF RELIQUIÆ WOTTONIANÆ.

1672.

[Reliquiæ

[Reliquiæ Wottonianæ: or a Collection of Lives, Letters, Poems; with Characters of Sundry Personages: and other Incomparable Pieces of Language and Art. Also Additional Letters to several Persons, not before Printed. By the Curious Pencil of the Ever Memorable Sir Henry Wotton, K*, Late Provost of Eaton Colledge. The Third Edition, with large Additions. London: Printed by T. Roycroft, for R. Marriott, F. Tyton, T. Collins, and J. Ford, 1672.]

To

WALTONIANA.

To the Right Honourable PHILIP Earl of Chesterfield, Lord Stanhop of Shelford.

My Lord,

I HAVE conceived many Reasons, why I ought in Justice to Dedicate these Reliques of Your Great Uncle, Sir Henry Wotton, to Your Lordship; some of which are, that both Your Grand-mother and Mother had a double Right to them by a Dedication when first made Publick; as also, for their assisting me then, and since, with many Material Informations for the Writing his Life; and for giving me many of the Letters that have fallen from his curious Pen : so that they being now dead, these Reliques descend to You, as Heir

to

to them, and the Inheritor of the memorable Bocton Palace, the Place of his Birth, where so many of the Ancient, and Prudent, and Valiant Family of the Wottons lie now Buried; whose remarkable Monuments You have lately Beautified, and to them added so many of so great Worth, as hath made it appear, that at the Erecting and Adorning them, You were above the thought of Charge, that they might, if possible, (for 'twas no easie undertaking) hold some proportion with the Merits of Your Ancestors.

My Lord, These are a part of many more Reasons that have inclin'd me to this Dedication; and these, with the Example of a Liberty that is not given, but now too usually taken by many Scriblers, to make trifling Dedications, might have begot a boldness in some Men of as mean as my mean Abilities to have undertaken this. But indeed, my Lord, though I was ambitious enough of undertaking it; yet, as Sir Henry Wotton hath
said

said in a Piece of his own Character, *That he was condemn'd by Nature to a bashfulness in making Requests*: so I find myself (pardon the Parallel) so like him in this, that if I had not had more Reasons then I have yet exprest, these alone had not been powerful enough to have created a Confidence in me to have attempted it. Two of my unexprest Reasons are, (*give me leave to tell them to Your Lordship and the World*) that Sir Henry Wotton, whose many Merits made him an Ornament even to Your Family, was yet so humble, as to acknowledge me to be his Friend; and died in a belief that I was so : since which time, I have made him the best return of my Gratitude for his Condescention, that I have been able to express, or he capable of receiving : and, am pleased with my self for so doing.

My other Reason of this boldness, is, an incouragement (*very like a command*) from Your worthy Cousin, and my Friend, *Mr. Charles Cotton,* who

who hath affured me, that You are fuch a Lover of the Memory of Your Generous Unkle, Sir Henry Wotton, that if there were no other Reafon then my endeavors to preferve it, yet, that that alone would fecure this Dedication from being un-acceptable.

I wifh, that nor he, nor I be miftaken; and that I were able to make You a more Worthy Prefent.

My Lord, I am and will be

Your Humble and moft

Affectionate Servant,

Izaak Walton.

Feb. 27, 1672.

LETTER

LETTER TO MARRIOTT.

1673.

G   [The

[The original is preferved in Corpus Chrifti College, Oxford, and was printed for the firft time in Sir Harris Nicolas' Life of Walton (Pickering, 1837), lxxix. lxxx.]

M^r.

WALTONIANA.

M^r. MARRIOTT,

I HAVE received Bentevolio, and in it M^r. Her^s. life; I thank you for both. I have since I saw you received from M^r. Milington so much of M^r. Hales his life as M^r. Faringdon had writ; and have made many inquiries concerning him of many that knew him, namely of M^{rs}. Powny, of Windsor, (at whose house he died), and as I have heard, so have set them down, that my memory might not lose them. M^r. Mountague did at my being in Windsor promise me to summon his memory, and set down what he knew of him. This I desired him to do at his best leisure, and write it down, and he that knew him and all his affairs best of any man is like to do it

very

very well, becaufe I think he will do it affectionately, fo that if M[r]. Fulman make his queries concerning that part of his life fpent in Oxford, he will have many, and good, I mean true informations from M[r]. Faringdon, till he came thither, and by me and my means fince he came to Eton.

This I write that you may inform M[r]. Fulman of it, and I pray let him know I will not yet give over my queries; and let him know that I hope to meet him and the Parliament in health and in London in October, and then and there deliver up my collections to him. In the mean time I wifh him and you health; and pray let him know it either by your writing to him, or fending him this of mine.

God keep us all in his favour,
his and your friend to ferve you,

IZAAK WALTON.

Winchefter, 24th Auguft, 1673.

PREFACE

PREFACE TO THEALMA AND

CLEARCHUS.

1678.

[Thealma

[Thealma and Clearchus, a Paſtoral Hiſtory, in ſmooth and
eaſie Verſe.   Written long ſince, By John Chalkhill, Eſq. ;
an Acquaintant and Friend of Edmund Spencer.   London :
Printed for Benj. Tooke, at the Ship in S. Paul's Church-yard,
1683.]

The

WALTONIANA.

The Preface.

THE Reader will find in this Book, what the Title declares, A Paſtoral Hiſtory, in ſmooth and eaſie Verſe; and will in it find many Hopes and Fears finely painted, and feelingly expreſſ'd. And he will find the firſt ſo often diſappointed, when fulleſt of deſire and expectation; and the later, ſo often, ſo ſtrangely, and ſo unexpectedly reliev'd, by an unforeſeen Providence, as may beget in him wonder and amazement.

And the Reader will here alſo meet with Paſſions heightned by eaſie and fit deſcriptions of Joy and Sorrow; and find alſo ſuch various events and rewards of innocent Truth and undiſſembled Honeſty

WALTONIANA.

Honefty, as is like to leave in him (if he be a good natur'd Reader) more fympathizing and virtuous Impreffions, than ten times fo much time fpent in impertinent, critical, and needlefs Difputes about Religion : and I heartily wifh it may do fo.

And, I have alfo this truth to fay of the Author, that he was in his time a man generally known, and as well belov'd ; for he was humble, and obliging in his behaviour, a Gentleman, a Scholar, very innocent and prudent : and indeed his whole life was ufeful, quiet, and virtuous. God fend the Story may meet with, or make all Readers like him.

I. W.*

May 7, 1678.

* The Poem of Thealma and Clearchus was left in an unfinifhed ftate: it terminates abruptly with the half line

              " Thealma lives "——

Upon which Walton adds

   And here the Author dy'd, and I hope the Reader will be forry.

LETTER

LETTER TO JOHN AUBREY.

1680.

[The

[The original is among Aubrey's MSS. in the Afhmolean
Mufeum : annexed to it is the following note by Aubrey:
" This account I received from Mr. Ifaac Walton (who wrote
" Dr. Donne's Life, &c. Decemb. 2, 1680, he being then
" eighty-feven years of age.   This is his own hand-writing,
" I.A."   *See Walton's Lives, With Notes and the Life of the
Author by Thomas Zouch, third edition.   York, 1817.   Vol. II.*
pp. 353-356.]

" ffor

" *ffor y*^r *ffriends q*^{ue} *this.*

I ONLY knew Ben Jonſon: But my Lord of Winton knew him very well; and ſays, he was in the 6°., that is, the uppermoſt fforme in Weſtminſter ſcole, at which time his father dyed, and his mother married a brickelayer, who made him (much againſt his will) help him in his trade; but in a ſhort time, his ſcolemaiſter, M^r. Camden, got him a better imployment, which was to atend or acompany a ſon of Sir Walter Rauley's in his travills. Within a ſhort time after their return, they parted (I think not in cole bloud) and with a love ſutable to what they had in their travilles (not to be commended). And then Ben began to ſet up for himſelf

felf in the trade by which he got his fubfiftance and fame, of which I need not give any account. He got in time to have a 100£ a yeare from the king, alfo a penfion from the cittie, and the like from many of the nobilitie and fome of the gentry, wᶜʰ was well pay'd, for love or fere of his railing in verfe, or profe, or boeth. My lord told me, he told him he was (in his long retyrement and ficknefs, when he faw him, which was often) much afflickted, that hee had profained the fcripture in his playes, and lamented it with horror : yet that, at that time of his long retyrement, his penfion (fo much as came in) was giuen to a woman that gouern'd him (with whome he liu'd and dyed near the Abie in Weftminfter) ; and that nether he nor fhe tooke too much care for next weike : and wood be fure not to want wine : of wᶜʰ he ufually tooke too much before he went to bed, if not oftener and foner. My lord tells me, he knowes not, but thinks he was born in Weftminfter. The queftion

queſtion may be put to M^r. Wood very eaſily upon what grounds he is poſitive as to his being born their; he is a friendly man, and will reſolve it. So much for braue Ben. You will not think the reſt ſo tedyous as I doe this.

ffor y^r 2 and 3 q^{ue} of M^r. Hill, and Bilingſley, I do neither know nor can learn any thing worth teling you.

for y^r two remaining q^{ue} of M^r. Warner, and M^r. Harriott this :

M^r. Warner did long and conſtantly lodg nere the water-ſtares, or market, in Woolſtable. Wool-ſtable is a place not far from Charing-Croſſe, and nerer to Northumberland-houſe. My lord of Wincheſter tells me, he knew him, and that he ſayde, he firſt found out the cerculation of the blood, and diſcover'd it to D^r. Haruie (who ſaid that 'twas he (himſelfe) that found it) for which he is ſo memorally famoſe. Warner had a penſion of 40l. a yeare from that Earle of Northumberland

that

that lay fo long a prifner in the Towre, and fom allowance from Sir Tho. Aylefbury, and with whom he ufually fpent his fumer in Windfor Park, and was welcom, for he was harmles and quet. His winter was fpent at the Woolftable, where he dyed in the time of the parlement of 1640, of which or whome, he was no louer.

M^r. Herriott, my lord tells me, he knew alfo: That he was a more gentile man than Warner. That he had 120£ a yeare penfion from the faid Earle (who was a louer of their ftudyes), and his lodgings in Syon-houfe, where he thinks, or believes, he dyed.

This is all I know or can learne for your friend; which I wifh may be worth the time and trouble of reading it.

I. W.

Nou^r. 22, 80.

IZAAK

IZAAK WALTON'S WILL.

1683.

WALTONIANA.

IN the name of God Amen. I Izaak Walton the elder of Winchester being this prefent day in the neintyeth yeare of my age and in perfect memory for wich prayfed be God : but Confidering how fodainly I may be deprived of boeth doe therfore make this my laft will and teftament as followeth. And firft I doe [declare] my beleife to be that their is only one God who hath made the whole world and me and all mankinde to whome I fhall give an acount of all my actions which are not to be juftified, but I hope pardoned for the merits of my faviour Jefus.—And becaufe [the

profeffion

profeffion of] Criftianity does at this time, feime to be fubdevided into papift and proteftant, I take it to be at leaft convenient to declare my beleife to be in all poynts of faith, as the Church of England now profeffeth. And this I doe the rather, becaufe of a very long and very trew friendfhip with fome of the Roman Church.

And for my worldly eftate, (which I have nether got by falfhood or flattery or the extreme crewelty of the law of this nation,) I doe hereby give and bequeth it as followeth.—Firft I give my fon-in-law Doc[r]. Hawkins and to his Wife, to them I give all my tytell and right of or in a part of a howfe and fhop in Pater-nofter-rowe in London : which I hold by leafe from the Lord Bifhop of London for about 50 years to come. and I doe alfo give to them all my right and tytell of or to a howfe in Chanfery-lane, London; where in M[rs]. Greinwood now dwelleth, in which is now about 16 years to come. I give thefe two leafes to them,
they

they faving my executor from all damage concerning the fame. (And I doe alfo give to my faide
dafter all my books this day at Winchefter and
Droxford : and what ever ells I can call mine their,
except a trunk of linen wch I give my fon Izaak
Walton. but if he doe not marry, or ufe the faide
linen himfelfe, then I give the fame to my grand-
doughter Anne Hawkins).

And I give to my fon Izaak, all my right and
tytell to a leafe of Norington farme, which I hold
from the lord B^p. of Winton.

And I doe alfo give him all my right and tytell
to a farme or land near to Stafford : which I
bought of M^r. Walter Noell : I fay, I give it to
him and [his] heares for ever. but upon the condition following. Namely—If my fone fhall not
marry before he fhall be of the age of forty and one
yeare ; or being marryed fhall dye before the faide
age and leve noe fon to inherit the faide farme or
land : or if his fon [or fonns] fhall not live to

ataine

ataine the age of twentie and one yeare, to difpofe
otherwayes of it, then I give the faide farme or
land to the towne or corperation of Stafford (in
which I was borne,) for the good and benifit of
fome of the faide towne, as I fhall direct and as followeth. but firft note, that it is at this prefant time
rented for 21ˡⁱ 10ˢ a yeare (and is like to hold the
faid rent, if care be taken to keipe the barne and
howfing in repaire) and I wood have and doe give
ten pownd of the faide rent, to binde out yearely
two boyes, the fons of honeft and pore parents to
be apprentices to fom tradefmen or handy-craft-
men, to the intent the faide boyes [may] the better
afterward get their owne living.—And I doe alfo
give five pownd yearly, out of the faid rent to be
given to fome meade-fervant, that hath atain'd the
age of twenty and [one] yeare (not les), and dwelt
long in one fervis, or to fom honeft pore man's
daughter, that hath atain'd to that age, to [be]
paide her, at or on the day of her marriage.

And

And this being done, my will is, that what rent ſhall remaine of the ſaide farme or land, ſhall be diſpoſed of as followeth.

Firſt I doe give twenty ſhillings yearely, to be ſpent by the maior of Stafford and thoſe that ſhall colect the ſaid rent : and diſpoſe of it as I have and ſhall hereafter direct. And that what mony or rent ſhall remaine undiſpoſed offe ſhall be imployed to buie coles for ſome pore people, that ſhall moſt neide them in the ſaid towne ; the ſaide coles to be delivered the laſt weike in Janewary, or in every firſt weike in Febrewary : I ſay then, becauſe I take that time to be the hardeſt and moſt pinching times with pore people. And God reward thoſe that ſhall doe this with out partialitie and with honeſtie and a good contience.

And if the ſaide maior and others of the ſaide towne of Stafford, ſhall prove ſo necligent or diſhoneſt as not to imploy the rent by me given as intended and expreſt in this my will, (which God

forbid,)

forbid,) then I give the faide rents and profits, of
the faide farme or land, to the towne and chiefe ma-
geftrats or governers of Ecles-hall, to be difpofed
by them in fuch maner as I have ordered the dif-
pofall of it, by the towne of Stafford. the faid
Farme or land being nere the towne of Ecles-hall.

And I give to my fon-in-law Doctor Hawkins,
(whome I love as my owne fon) and to my dafter
his wife, and my fon Izaak to each of them a ring
with thefe words or motto;—love my memory,
I. W. obiet = to the Lord B^p of Winton a ring
with this motto—a mite for a million : I. W.
obiet =" And to the freinds hearafter named I
give to each of them a ring with this motto A
friends farewell. I. W. obiet" = and my will is,
the faid rings be delivered within fortie dayes of
my deth. and that the price or valew of all the
faide rings fhall be—1 3^s 4^d a peice.

I give to Doctor Hawkins Docto^r Donns Sermons; which I have hear'd preacht, and read with
much

much content. to my fon Izaak I give Doc[r] Sibbs
his *Soules Conflict*, and to my doughter his *Brewfed
Reide*; defiring them to reade them fo, as to be
well aquanted with them. and I alfo give to her
all my bookes at Winchefter and Droxford, and
what ever in thofe two places are or I can call
mine : except a trunk of linen, which I gave to
my fon Izaak, but if he doe not live to make ufe
of it, then I give the fame to my grand-dafter,
Anne Hawkins : And I give my dafter Doc[r] Halls
Works which be now at Farnham.

To my fon Izaak I give all my books, (not yet
given) at Farnham Caftell and a defke of prints
and pickters; alfo a cabinet nere my beds head, in
w[ch] are fom littell things that he will valew, tho of
noe great worth.

And my will and defyre is, that he will be kind
to his Ante Beacham and his ant Rofe Ken : by
alowing the firft about fiftie fhilling a yeare in or
for bacon and cheife (not more), and paying 4[li] a
yeare

---

yeare toward the bordin of her fon's dyut to Mʳ. John Whitehead. for his ante Ken, I defyre him to be kinde to her according to her neceflitie and his owne abillitie. and I comend one of her children to breide up (as I have faide I intend to doe) if he fhall be able to doe it. as I know he will ; for, they be good folke.

I give to Mʳ. John Darbifhire the Sermons of Mʳ. Antony Faringdon, or of doʳ Sanderfon, which my executor thinks fit. to my fervant, Thomas Edghill I give five pownd in mony, and all my clothes linen and wollen except one fute of clothes, (which I give to Mʳ. Holinfhed, and forty fhiling) if the faide Thomas be my fervant at my deth, if not my cloths only.

And I give my old friend Mʳ. Richard Marriot ten pownd in mony, to be paid him within . 3 . months after my deth. and I defyre my fon to fhew kindenes to him if he fhall neide, and my fon can fpare it.

And

WALTONIANA.

And I doe hereby will and declare my fon Izaak to be my fole executo^r of this my laſt will and teſtament; and Do^r Hawkins, to fee that he performs it, which I doubt not but he will.

I defyre my buriall may be nere the place of my deth; and free from any oſtentation or charg, but privately : this I make to be my laſt will, (to which I only add the codicell for rings,) this 16. day of Auguſt, 1683.

Witnes to this will.   IZAAK WALTON.

The rings I give are as on the other fide.

To my brother Jon Ken.	to my brother Beacham.
to my fiſter his wife.	to my fiſter his wife.
to my brother Doc^r Ken.	to the lady Anne How.
to my fiſter Pye.	to M^rs. King Do^r Philips wife.
to M^r. Francis Morley.	to M^r. Valantine Harecourt.
to Sr George Vernon.	to M^rs. Elyza Johnſon.
to his wife.	to M^rs. Mary Rogers.
to his 3 dafters.	to M^rs. Elyza Milward.
to M^rs. Nelſon.	to M^rs. Doro. Wallop.

 to

to M^r. Rich. Walton.
to M^r. Palmer.
to M^r. Taylor.
to M^r. Tho. Garrard.
to the Lord B^p. of Sarum.
to M^r. Rede his Servant.
to my Coz. Dorothy Kenrick.
to my Coz. Lewin.
to M^r. Walter Higgs.
to M^r. Cha Cotton.
to M^r. Rich. Marryot.

to M^r. Will. Milward of
Chrift-Church, Oxford.
to M^r. John Darbefhire.
to M^r. Veudvill.
to M^{rs}. Rock.
to M^r. Peter White.
to M^r. John Lloyde.
to my Coz Greinfells
— widow
16 M^{rs}. Dalbin muft not
be forgotten.

22

Note that feveral lines are blotted
out of this will for they are twice
repeted : And, that this will is now
figned & fealed, this twenty and
fourth day of October 1683 in the
prefence of us— } Izaak Walton

Witnes, Abra. Markland.
Jos : Taylor,
Thomas Crawley.